MISTER TOAD

by Clyde Watson
illustrations by N. Cameron Watson

MACMILLAN PUBLISHING COMPANY   NEW YORK

MAXWELL MACMILLAN CANADA   TORONTO

MAXWELL MACMILLAN INTERNATIONAL   NEW YORK   OXFORD   SINGAPORE   SYDNEY

Macmillan Publishing Company is part of the Maxwell
Communication Group of Companies.

Macmillan Publishing Company
866 Third Avenue
New York, NY 10022

Maxwell Macmillan Canada, Inc.
1200 Eglinton Avenue East
Suite 200
Don Mills, Ontario M3C 3N1

First edition. Printed in Hong Kong by South China Printing
Company (1988) Ltd.

10   9   8   7   6   5   4   3   2   1

The text of this book is set in 14 pt. ITC Berkeley Old Style.
The illustrations are rendered in watercolor.

Library of Congress Cataloging-in-Publication Data
Watson, Clyde.
Mister Toad / by Clyde Watson ; illustrations by N.
Cameron Watson. — 1st ed.
        p.   cm.
Summary: Mister Toad loves his house inside a stone wall,
until it is invaded by unwanted visitors.
ISBN 0-02-792527-7
[1. Toads—Fiction.   2. Cats—Fiction.   3. Bees—Fiction.]
I. Watson, N. Cameron (Nancy Cameron) ill.   II. Title.
III. Title: Mr. Toad.
PZ7.W3263Mi   1992   [E]—dc20   91-24208

for Dad

Mister T. Tamson Toad puffed heavily as he hurried in the door and banged it shut behind him. Out of breath and annoyed, he went to the kitchen and put the kettle on to boil. Then he stood in the middle of the kitchen floor, tapping his foot and frowning.

"What a fine how d'ya do!" he muttered to himself.

This was Mister Toad's favorite time of day, but his peaceful early morning walk had just been rudely interrupted by an inconsiderate neighbor, a certain Miss Kitty, who had chased him right to his own doorstep. He had gotten in just in the nick of time.

"It's disgraceful," he continued angrily. "Can't a person be left in peace anymore?"

Mister Toad lived in the flower garden at old Mrs. Quimby's. His home was in a hollow place inside the stone wall. He had a large, sunny living room looking out onto the garden, a small kitchen at the back, and a tiny bedroom off to one side. The well-kept front lawn was lovely for early morning outings, with little stone pathways winding through beds of Virginia bluebells, forget-me-nots, pinks, and daisies. Though Mrs. Quimby did her share of the garden work, Mister Toad always called it *his* garden.

Still frowning and shaking his head, Mister Toad made himself a pot of acorn tea, and proceeded to the living room. At least he could enjoy the remainder of the sunrise through the window, he thought to himself ruefully.

But as he sat there, the situation continued to bother him. Things were…changing so much lately. There were too many newcomers: a young bachelor toad straight from the city, spouting new-fangled ideas and language; a rowdy swarm of bees, always looking for new lodgings on other people's property; and of course, Charlie Chatter of Nutt Developers, agitating to build a twelve-unit condo in the ancient pine over Mrs. Quimby's garden.

But in Mister Toad's opinion, this Miss Kitty was the most unpleasant addition to the community. She was a saucy young thing, just past the kitten stage, who would chase anything that moved. Mister Toad had found her amusing at first—chuckling at the way she pounced on blowing leaves and dry twigs—but just last week she had caught a friend of his, Abby Deermouse, who hadn't been heard from since. Now that the cat knew where *he* lived, thought Mister Toad, things would surely get worse.

The very next afternoon, Mister Toad was relaxing in his favorite living room chair, reading the newspaper and enjoying his third cup of acorn tea with honey.

He knew very well that Miss Kitty was lying in the sun on his roof, because every time he turned a page or rustled the paper the least little bit, he could see her tail switch past the window, back and forth.

At the moment, he didn't care that much—it was when he wished to go out, and couldn't, that he really resented the cat. Just now he felt quite content to read the paper in the safety of his living room. True, he *had* moved his chair away from the window, which could not be shut— but only just in case.

Now, all of a sudden, a shadow darkened the room, and looking up, Mister Toad could see something glowing green-gold at the window. He realized it was the cat's eye. He could hear her noisy, excited breathing—now what?

Before he could think what to do, she poked her big white paw right through the window and into the room, claws out.

Mister Toad sat stuck in his chair, unable to move. With a series of little jerks, the paw came further and further into the room, groping the air, knocking over chairs, ripping pictures off the walls—it even tipped over the tea table, tray and all!

Luckily, Mister Toad's chair was just out of reach, but those sharp claws came way too close for comfort.

Finding nothing she could really get ahold of, the cat finally withdrew her paw and went back to the roof, where she lay twitching her tail and waiting. Mister Toad, his peace shattered, took the paper and retreated to the kitchen.

"This is the last straw!" he croaked. "Something will *have* to be done!"

He poured himself a fresh cup of tea with trembling hands.

"I do *not* intend to move," he went on. "I have lived here *always,* and I refuse to be forced out of my own house by a mere CAT!"

As if the last five minutes had not been upsetting enough, a new predicament now arose. A large, rude bee—the Queen, judging from her behavior—suddenly flew into his kitchen without even knocking.

"I hear you might have a room to spare," announced the Queen, settling herself on the edge of the honey pot and taking a lick.

"No, you are mistaken," replied Mister Toad stiffly. "No such thing. I've never taken in boarders—and I do not mean to begin now."

"It needn't be fancy," remarked the Queen, dipping her disgusting long tongue into Mister Toad's honey pot again. "Just enough room for myself and my entourage." She waved her lacy wing toward the living room, where Mister Toad could see her swarm of attendants bumbling around, already starting to make themselves at home amongst his things.

The toad stood silent for a moment, truly shaken by the day's events. He realized that if the Queen took it into her head to move in without his permission, there was not a single thing he could do about it.

He was just going to say "no" again, more firmly than before, when a new and clever idea—quite unusual for Mister Toad—entered his head.

"Well, Your Majesty," he said slowly, "Perhaps I *could* rent you the front living room. It's really the only room large enough for all of you," he added. "Just give me an hour or so to arrange things."

So Mister Toad moved his best belongings out of the living room and into the little back bedroom—and then in came the bees, buzzing and whirring endlessly as they settled themselves in their new quarters.

"You may keep the honey pot here in your room," offered Mister Toad generously, making a note in his mind to wash it thoroughly before he ever used it again.

And then he went to bed with his bedroom door shut, curiously content and rather looking forward to the next day.

The sun was up on time, but the morning passed slowly. Mister Toad went out briefly first thing, and had breakfast in the daisies. Miss Kitty was nowhere to be seen, and it was a beautiful day, but Mister Toad was much too edgy to enjoy it. He returned to the house and sat in the kitchen, drumming his fingers on the table and wondering if he had done the right thing after all by renting his living room to all those bees. The day was already growing warm, and Mister Toad was very tired of their annoying buzzing and the constant coming and going.

Then, along about noon, things began to happen. Miss Kitty was let out of the big house, and sure enough, along she came on soft white paws to wish Mister Toad a good day. He could hear her sniffing around outside his house, and then suddenly—

The paw! There it was, just coming in the window! It disappeared briefly, and the green-gold eye appeared in its place. The sight and the sound of all those bees must have excited Miss Kitty more than usual, for she gave several uncontrolled little squeals and stuck her paw in again—further this time—and began batting it around. This excited the bees tremendously; they began to swarm all around the paw, growing more and more angry. Finally, several especially brave bees landed on the waving paw, and nestled down into the fur.

Two seconds later, the paw gave a jump and hit the ceiling; then, accompanied by a very loud *MEO-OOW*, it disappeared out the window. A number of furious bees zoomed out after it and chased Miss Kitty across the lawn. Other bees stayed behind, flying about in terror and bumping into things.

The Queen stalked angrily into the kitchen, where Mister Toad had been watching the goings-on.

"We shall *not* be staying after all!" she announced in a rage. "The neighborhood is *not* suitable!"

"I'm *so* sorry," murmured Mister Toad innocently, from behind his teacup.

"And I shan't pay a *minute's* rent!" said the Queen, stamping her foot.

"Certainly not!" agreed Mister Toad soothingly. "I wouldn't expect you to."

The Queen stormed out, followed by the rest of the bees. As the last one flew away, buzz and confusion subsided into a lovely stillness. Mister Toad looked around at the wreckage of his living room.

"Nothing too terrible, luckily," he thought, and whistling to himself, he began to pick up broken china and put furniture back into place.

As for Miss Kitty, Mister Toad looked out and saw her sitting a respectful distance away from his house, tenderly licking a *very* large and puffy paw as she looked reproachfully in his direction.

Mister Toad washed out his honey pot, dried it, and filled it with fresh, new honey.

"Now perhaps I shall have some peace and quiet again!" he sighed, as he settled into his best chair and put his feet up.